FEATHERS

Be Blessed.

FEATHERS

This Woman, My Mother:
A Monologue

By
Pamela Watson

All scripture cited herein was taken from the King James Version Bible.

ISBN: 1-58597-251-7

Library of Congress Control Number: 2004100241

A division of Squire Publishers, Inc.
4500 College Blvd.
Leawood, KS 66211
1/888/888-7696
www.leatherspublishing.com

ACKNOWLEDGMENT

Special thanks to Joanna Smith,
author of "Missing Pieces," 1989.

DEDICATION

I dedicate this book with love and with understanding, to my mother and my three children whom I adore. Also to a special lady and friend that I met in August of 2000, named Connie Beshore, for the encouragement that I received from her, to write a book for children within the foster care system.

To the thousands of children in our society who have chosen to run away, and those who were placed in foster care because of abuse and neglect within their own families, I encourage you to stay strong, and to love yourself always. But most of all to seek and find your strength from the Lord. It tells us in the book of *Philippians 4:13 "... I can do all things through Christ which strengthens me."*

I found the Lord and my Saviour Jesus Christ at the early age of nine years old, and learned to believe in His word that He would always protect and guide me. I know this because God said it in the book of *Proverbs 3:5-6: "Trust in the Lord with all thine heart; and lean not unto thine own understanding. In all thy ways acknowledge him, and he shall direct thy paths."*

TABLE OF CONTENTS

INTRODUCTION

Growing up with relatives after the death of her parents, Penny finds the strength to survive as a young child by building an emotional barrier of hate as protection.

After years of resentful feelings for "this woman, my mother," she finally comes to terms with her unhappy childhood, and what has happened between the two of them to accept the one gift that is given to her — the ability to survive. Throughout her childhood, Penny is inflicted with physical, emotional and sexual abuse. Despite all the abuse and a teenage pregnancy, she perseveres, graduates from high school in the top of her class, and, above all, learns that this woman, her mother, truly loves her.

This story is a fictionalized account of actual events, with the names and places changed to protect all those involved. It is also a call for help for so many children who have been hushed by fear of abandonment, or left to languish in our foster care system. Unfortunately, some have been silenced forever and their cries left unheard …

I

"For he saith, I have heard thee in a time accepted, and in the day of salvation have I succoured thee: behold, now is the accepted time; behold, now is the day of salvation."
— *II Corinthians 6:2*

This Woman, My Mother

THE TELEPHONE RANG and I knew even before I answered it who the caller would be on the other end. The call was not unexpected; it was somewhat a welcome to an end.

It had only been less than eight hours since I had left that place that I had grown accustomed to calling my home. Every Friday evening as soon as I arrived home from work, my youngest daughter Melanie would be waiting for me with the overnight bags packed, and was ready to go to that place I called home. *Home.* Back home once again, to visit this woman, my mother, who had raised me as her own child at the age of four years old, and who now was lying quietly, crumpled up in pain, but never complaining, in an old hospital bed. Although in pain she lay there quietly, almost peaceful looking, while enduring the war within her, as she was slowly losing the battle of cancer that daily ate away and rapidly invaded all of the living organs in her now very frail body.

A loving smile directed at me from this woman, my mother, and I a kiss lightly to her forehead, as I sat on the edge of her hospital bed. I felt useless. There was nothing that I could do or say to help ease her pain. The look she gave me, with the slight nod of her head, was an acknowledgment to me of how much she truly loved me as her daughter. I realized now at this moment and understood that the unsaid words in the past were now unnecessary from her. Words that I had needed to hear from her through the years as a child growing up in her home feeling unloved. This moment with her was enough now for the things that had been done in the past, now could be buried in the past. It was now finally enough for me to know that I truly loved this woman, my mother, as my Mother. This moment with her was a loving and peaceful togetherness, for the first time between a mother and a daughter. Together in silence we, as mother and daughter, finally accepted a quiet forgiveness from each other.

Sighing, I thought that this was an end to a release of bottled-up emotions, a release of obligation to love out of duty, a release from years of built-up rage and hatred that had been quietly controlled and hidden away, but never forgotten. A final release to the shedding of all things that happened decades in the past, that had been frozen in the back of the my mind, yet unclaimed. Releases for a long-awaited and welcomed exhale.

I held her hand while sitting at her bedside until she closed her eyes to rest. Slowly she drifted off to sleep, and I moved to the old worn recliner in the corner of the cold hospital room. Soon, I too drifted off to sleep as I closed my eyes to rest. While I slept, I began to recall some of those memories as they suddenly drifted back into my mind.

The memories came slowly at first, then rapidly came exploding forward into my mind and head so quickly that I began to feel as if I was drowning. I was drowning in the flood of my own memories, as if it were only yesterday. I saw myself at three years old, and I smiled, as I recalled the memory of when I was in a hospital, a long time ago, frightened as a little child.

▐▐

"An ungodly witness scorneth judgment: and the mouth of the wicked devoureth iniquity. Judgments are prepared for scorners, and stripes for the back of fools."

— Proverbs 19:28-29

My Uncle's House

SMILING AS THE pleasant, yet painful memory comes back to me of my big brother Geronimo. He was really named after my daddy, but because he liked to play cowboys and Indians so much, he was nicknamed "Geronimo." He never liked playing the part of the Indian, although everyone said he acted like a wild savage Indian all the time, because of the Indian blood that runs in our veins. Nevertheless, my big brother Geronimo was always especially nice to me the time I hurt my tongue on a broken faucet and had to go to the hospital to get stitches.

We had been visiting at our Uncle Arthur's house playing with our cousins, Jamie, Caroline, Kevin and Stephen. They acted mean and hateful to us sometimes, as if they were better than we were. We had fun playing with them anyway, at least most of the time anyway. They lived in a nice house, and the girls and boys did not have to share a bedroom. Their dad was always doing some kind of remodeling around the house.

"You kids stop that running through the house before someone gets hurt," yelled Aunt Mavis, who was their mother. She was a very small woman, like our mommy, only she could yell loud.

"Yes, ma'am," we all chimed in chorus.

But that only lasted a few seconds until the next tag game, started by our cousin Jamie by hitting me on the top of my head, and yelling "Tag, you're it. Penny." Off they all went, running away to hide from me.

"One, two, three, four, five, ready or not, here I come. Geronimo, where are you," I yell, after searching behind the chairs, the curtains in the bedroom and in the closets for them. "Not fair, you guys, I can't find any of you," I cried.

"Oh, okay, here I am, Penny, I'll be it for you," Geronimo said, not wanting to hear me cry.

"Geronimo, that's not fair, you can't take her turn. She's just a big cry baby," Jamie yelled.

"Don't you talk about my sister, or I'll beat you up," Geronimo screamed at our cousin Jamie with his hands in a tight fist.

"Okay, okay. Come on, you guys, stop fussing before we all get in trouble from Father and Mother," said Caroline, who was Jamie's younger sister. I thought they were so well-mannered and proper speaking, saying Father and Mother instead of Daddy and Mommy, all the time when referring to their parents. "Anyway, I'm thirsty, let's get some water in Mother's bathroom," she continued. We followed our cousins into the big bathroom that was still being remodeled by their father, *along with the rest of the house it seemed*, through their parents' bedroom.

"You guys, Uncle Arthur said not to play around in here, or go into their bathroom. We're going to get a whipping," I warned them. I had seen Uncle Arthur use his long razor strap on his oldest son Stephen and my big brother Geronimo. I sure did not want to get a whipping from him with that razor strap. My mommy had screamed to make him stop whipping her child, my big brother, or else she would call the police on him when he did this.

"Be quiet, Penny, and come on if you want a drink. Besides, we do not get whippings. We're not bad like you and Geronimo," Jamie said.

"Be quiet Jamie. I only get whippings when I'm around you guys, because you all tell lies on me all the time," Geronimo said.

Jamie and the rest of our cousins just ignored us, proceeded on into their parents' bathroom anyway, without responding to either of us, and knowingly disobeying their parents.

"It's all right, Penny. Come on, I'm going with you, and I'm thirsty, too," Geronimo said, grabbing hold of my hand.

"Wow!" I exclaimed as I entered the bathroom tagging behind the others.

I was only three and half years old, but I already had a keen eye for beautiful things and knew what was pretty or just plain looking. This really was going to be a beautiful bathroom, once it was finally completed. "Boy, can our uncle do some nice building on stuff," I whispered to my big brother. I didn't want my cousins, especially Jamie, to hear me, or else she'd think that I thought their parents' bathroom was pretty, and better than our bathroom at our small house on the other side of town. That would just make her boast again about how much better stuff they had than we did again. Still, I just could not keep from looking around at everything. This just had to be the biggest makings of a bathroom that I have ever seen in my life. Although I had not seen many bathrooms, except in the magazines that my mommy bought at the store.

There were no little cups in the holder that has been attached to the side of the medicine cabinet, so everyone was taking turns bending their heads under the faucet opening to get a drink of water. They were all bigger than me, so I had to stand on a nearby stool that my big brother pulled over, and he helped me up to the faucet for my turn to get a drink.

Just as I put my mouth under the faucet, the sink started to wobble and the stool slipped from under my feet. I lost my balance, knocking my big brother down, and I came falling down on top of him with the cold water handle and the faucet broken off and stuck in my mouth. Geronimo, scrambling from under me, saw the sink as it was starting to fall toward me and tried to catch it before it hit me in the face. He was too late. The whole sink and part of the plaster on the wall came crashing down on top of me, and the hot water handle that was still attached to the sink struck me so hard in the face, it hit my mouth and front teeth like cold steel. Blood was gushing out everywhere, and all I could hear was myself, screaming at the sight of all the blood, and from the pain, and knew that I must have died.

My cousins, running from the accident scene in the bathroom, were yelling for their mother and father. Running away to tattle on my big brother and me for disobeying them by entering into the bathroom, after being told not to go in there.

"Mother, Father, hurry, hurry. Geronimo and Penny were in your bathroom, even after Father said to stay out of there," said Jamie, implying that we were alone in this escapade. "And they broke your sink and everything, and Penny has blood all over her. And we told them not to go in there and stuff, but they did it anyway," Jamie continued out of breath.

"You guys are lying. Always trying to get somebody in trouble," Geronimo yelled over my head almost in tears. "Penny is hurt real bad. Hurry, I think she's dying."

Our mommy, hearing my screams, pushed past everyone and was in the bathroom beside me, and then gasped loudly, putting her hands to her mouth when she saw me covered with my blood. "Oh, my god, Skipper, get here quick," she screamed to my daddy. "Hurry, somebody call the ambulance now, and the doctor, hurry," she shouted.

Seconds later my daddy was kneeling down beside

my mommy and me. "My God, what happened here?" he asked angrily, looking from my big brother Geronimo to his brother's children. Not waiting for a response, he turned to my mommy. "Forget the ambulance, it will be quicker, Joan, if we drive her to the hospital ourselves. Calm down and get me some clean towels." Then back to his brother's kids, he yelled for them to move out of the way, and then to his brother, "Arthur, pull the car around," he said loudly, with a direct calmness to his voice, as my uncle was still trying to shoo his precious children out of the bathroom. My mommy was getting clean towels from Aunt Mavis' linen closet, and I was lying there on the floor soaking with blood and still crying at the top of my lungs, not calm at all. My big brother Geronimo was still sitting there beside me, with tears in his eyes, and holding my hand.

"It's okay, Penny, don't cry. Daddy knows what to do, he is a police officer, and he knows everything. He's seen even worse stuff than this, it'll be all right, Penny, you'll see," he said, trying his best to convince himself more than me.

My daddy gently scooped me up in his arms with the towels pushed close into my mouth and around my bloody face. He rushed out of the bathroom through the bedroom and through the rest of the house, then out to the outside of the garage and into the running car parked in the driveway, where my Uncle Arthur was waiting for us behind the steering wheel. My mommy and Geronimo were right behind my daddy and me. Uncle Arthur, seeing Geronimo, yelled at him to stay with the rest of the kids and Aunt Mavis. The harshness of his voice was indicative of the actions he was already planning for later for my big brother for disobeying his rules. Geronimo just ignored him and climbed into the car behind our mommy anyway.

"I have to go with Penny or else she'll be scared of the doctors and having to go to the hospital," Geronimo said very firmly, slamming the car door behind him. "I have to go with her and hold her hand; besides, it's my fault. Because I didn't hold her good on the stool, and now she might even die."

"He's okay, Arthur. You just drive this car as fast as you can to the hospital," my mommy ordered Uncle Arthur, and then turning assuredly to my big brother, "Honey, it is not your fault, it was an accident. The sink was already broken, and it could have fallen on any one of you kids. Penny is not going to die and will be just fine, you'll see."

And I was just fine, after emergency surgery on my mouth that included several stitches to my tongue, the roof of my mouth, and the necessary removal of my two front baby teeth that had been broken off in my gums. The doctors would not guarantee my mommy and daddy if my front teeth would ever grow back properly because of the damage to the nerves. I would probably have to have artificial teeth or something.

It seemed as if it took forever before I was completely recuperated from my accident. Our mommy dared not let any of us kids out of her sight again for fear of another accident to one of her precious children.

III

"Yea, they sacrificed their sons and their daughters unto devils, and shed innocent blood, even the blood of their sons and of their daughters, whom they sacrificed unto the idols of Canaan: and the land was polluted with blood."
— *Psalms 106:37-38*

Mr. Crutchfield

IT WAS A bright, sunny Saturday afternoon, and our daddy was working in the driveway on the old station wagon we owned. My big brother Geronimo and I were finally allowed to go out into the front of the house to play. We played hard and long for all the days we had missed from playing outside. We played on the old tire swing that was hanging from the big oak tree that was in the front of the house. We played cowboy and Indian, and then my big brother Geronimo fed me black ants that he caught crawling on the sidewalk. He laughed at the funny faces I made when swallowing the ants.

I soon tired quickly of the ant feast, and we played more cowboy and Indian again, because this was Geronimo's favorite game. I was always the Indian, of course, and he was the lone cowboy. He had a big red cowboy hat with a black and white band around it, and a shiny pair of black and white cowboy boots. Our mommy had ironed his red plaid shirt and blue jeans with the cuffs for him to wear that day. I thought he was the cutest big brother and cowboy I had ever seen. He always won at cowboy and Indian, too, but I did not care. Sometimes he would let me win if I started to cry, and would even let me shoot his cap gun. All I had was two old dry sticks, one that he had tied a rubber band on to use as a bow, and the other as an arrow for my weapon.

"Hey, look, Penny. It's Mr. Crutchfield riding on his horse," exclaimed Geronimo, jumping up and down excitedly, after I had just shot him dead with his cap gun. "Daddy, Daddy, look. Here comes Mr. Crutchfield. Can we ride the horse? Oh please, Daddy, I'll be good if you let me."

I also had seen old Mr. Crutchfield, riding on his big brown horse down the street toward our house. I pretended not to see him, and I went back to the old tire swing and tried ignoring my big brother as he pleaded with our daddy.

Old Mr. Crutchfield was a retired police officer and considered a nice old white man. He and my daddy talked about police stuff whenever he came around. He lived on the other side of town, but always came over to our neighborhood on the weekends, and would give all the kids rides on his big brown horse. All the kids and parents liked him and thought he was such a nice old man who took up his weekend just to give pleasure to their children by giving them horseback rides. One by one, all the neighborhood children would line up for a ride on the big brown horse. Up and down the block and back again.

However, I did not like him very much, I even hated him. I knew a secret that others did not know about him. Secrets that he made me keep only between the two of us. Therefore, I did not tell anyone. I did not even tell my big brother Geronimo. Mr. Crutchfield told me never to tell anyone, or else he would never give my big brother rides again on his big brown horse. I loved my big brother too much to disappoint him, so I never told. However, I knew that Mr. Crutchfield was not a nice old man as everyone thought. If they only knew of the things he did to little girls like me, they would hate him, too.

This bright and sunny Saturday afternoon he came only to our house. He wanted to chit-chat with our daddy about police stuff again, as he watched him work on his car. Geronimo, still admiring the big brown horse, began to beg and plead again with our daddy if he could get a ride. Finally, after talking and finishing up fiddling with the car, Mr. Crutchfield turned and asked our daddy if it was all right to give us kids a quick ride before he left. My daddy, knowing what a nice old man Mr. Crutchfield was, gave in to him and my big brother's pleas, and helped Geronimo up into the front of the saddle on the horse. I kept swinging on the old tire and trying to ignore all that was going on. After they are out of sight, I went and sat on the porch in front of the house to wait for my big brother to get back from his ride. It seemed like forever that they were gone.

"Daddy, when will they be back?" I asked. "I want my big brother to play with."

"Be patient, Penny, you will get your turn," my father said.

"I don't want a turn, Daddy, I just want my big brother back here now," I exclaimed.

"Well, look over there, Penny, here they come now," Daddy said.

I start to wave to my brother sitting on top of that big brown horse, looking like a real cowboy we see on the television, but smaller.

"Now it's your turn, Penny," smiled Mr. Crutchfield, winking at me as he lowered Geronimo to the ground off his big brown horse.

"No, sir, thank you. I don't want to ride the horse today," I protested, starting to cry.

"Of course you do. You couldn't wait until they got back," my daddy said, laughing.

"But not to ride, Daddy, I just wanted my big brother back."

"Oh, go on, Penny, don't be a crybaby. The horse won't hurt you, it's fun, and Mr. Crutchfield will let you hold the reins," Geronimo said, reassuring me, still excited from his ride.

"Oh, all right, Geronimo." Daddy was already helping me onto the saddle on top of the big brown horse in front of Mr. Crutchfield.

"They're coming back, Daddy, look," yelled Geronimo as he ran toward the end of the driveway.

Returning from my horseback ride, I quickly wiped my eyes as I get closer to our house. Mr. Crutchfield lowered me to the ground from the big brown horse, and I ran straight to the porch and sat down, not thanking the nice old man for the ride.

"What's the matter, Penny?" my big brother questioned me. "Didn't you like the ride?"

Our daddy just smiled as he looked at me, and then back to Mr. Crutchfield, saying "I don't think she likes horses much. Not like her brother anyway. He is a born cowboy," he boasted with admiration for his oldest son.

"Oh, she'll be just fine. She'll get used to it sooner or later," Mr. Crutchfield said as he rode away on his big brown horse, down the street and back to the other side of town where he belonged, with a smile on his face.

IV

"The sorrows of death compassed me, and the floods of ungodly men made me afraid. The sorrows of hell compassed me about: the snares of death prevented me. In my distress I called upon the Lord, and cried unto my God; he heard my voice out of his temple, and my cry came before him, even into his ears. — *Psalms 18:4-6*

Mommy

AN ON-DUTY NURSE had come into the hospital room to check this woman, my mother. Although the nurse was very quiet in her movements about the room, not wanting to not disturb this woman, my mother, or me, I could still sense her presence. Once she had left the room, I too checked to make sure this woman, my mother, was as comfortable as possible. Gazing down at her, I saw in the wrinkles of her brow all the pain and suffering she had endured in her life, upon her face. Gently I caressed her face and rubbed the loose gray hairs from her forehead. I returned back to my old worn recliner in the corner of the hospital room, and to the memories of that same peacefulness I once saw on my mommy's face ...

"Mommy, wake up. Mommy, please wake up," cried the wide-eyed four-year-old Penny as she shook her sleeping mother. 'Geronimo, hurry and come here. Mommy will not wake up. I think she is playing a game with us again'."

"Hold on, Penny. I'll be there in a minute."

"But I'm hungry and the baby won't stop crying. And Junio is stinky again, and Cassie won't come out of the closet."

"You guys just hold on and be quiet, I said," Geronimo answered from the bathroom. He always goes in there as soon as Daddy leaves the house. He doesn't think I know what he is doing, but I peeked in one morning and watched him as he went through the same routine that our daddy did every morning before he leaves for work. First, he puts all this white soapy stuff all over his face and then he sits on the edge of the toilet pretending to go, but he doesn't. He pulls a pack of cigarettes out of his pocket and smokes it, blowing perfect little circles in the air. After he has finished his cigarette he flushes it down the toilet and proceeds to lather up the soap on his bare face and then takes the razor from the medicine cabinet and rubs it over his face. He then takes the washcloth that is soaking in the sink and holds it to his face. He checks himself thoroughly in the mirror, and after brushing his hair and teeth, remembers to spray the air freshener and emerges from the bathroom.

"I'm the man of the house now that Daddy is gone to work, so you all have to listen to me. Now keep quiet so Mommy can sleep, Penny. She's just a little tiréd, I heard the baby crying all night long. Stop shaking her, and I'll fix you guys some breakfast," Geronimo said, acting all grown up.

"Umm, you gonna get in trouble. You know what happened the last time you tried to fix breakfast," I warned. "You made a big mess and Daddy said you had to ask first before touching that stove again. You might get burnt or worse," I cried.

"Well, Daddy isn't here and Mommy is asleep. So if you want breakfast you better be quiet or else you have to wait until Mommy wakes up," Geronimo said.

I always gave in to Geronimo. After all, he was my big brother, although he was only eleven months older than I was. My big brother, Geronimo, was real smart and strong, too. Nobody messed with him, not even our other cousins that lived on the other side of town, and they were lots older.

"Okay," I said, turning to get Cassie and Junio. "Come on, Cassie, it's time to eat. You can come out of the closet now." I tried to get our little sister Cassie to come out of the closet, but she just sat there picking her nose as usual, unaware of anything going on, or anyone else besides herself. The little "princess" as everyone calls her. I just thought she was acting like a prissy butt and was a crybaby. I finally coaxed Cassie out of the closet, grabbed Junio by hand and headed to the kitchen.

My big brother was pouring milk from the sealed container he had pulled out of the refrigerator into a glass baby bottle. He had watched our mommy do this many times before, so he knew what to do. He set the bottle in a small pan on the stove and lit a match. He was good at lighting matches and cigarette lighters. However, he sometimes lit stuff he was not supposed to be lighting, especially when Daddy and Mommy were not around. I never told though, because he was my big brother and always shared everything with me. No matter what it was — candy, toys, or even the creepy, crawly black ants he found. Of course, he never ate the ants, just caught them and fed them to me instead. He told me they were good for me and would make me strong like him.

Once the bottle was warm, Geronimo got the crying baby Brandon from his crib, laid him on the bed beside our sleeping mommy, and propped the bottle in his mouth, just like he had seen our mommy do. He changed Brandon's diaper and left him to slurp quietly on his bottle. He hauled the rest of us kids, three-year-old Cassie, who was such a crybaby sissy, and one-year-old Junio, who was just barely walking, back into the small kitchen. Then he fed us a feast of bread with butter and lots of sugar and a glass of icy cold milk. We each got a graham cracker for drinking all our milk. Afterwards we all followed Geronimo back into our mother's bedroom and got into the bed with her and our baby brother Brandon who was now fast asleep. Our mommy looked so pretty lying there sleeping, yet almost awake with one eye open and the other closed.

"Hey, Geronimo, look, Mommy isn't really sleeping, she's just playing a game with us. See, look, she's got one eye open watching us."

"I said be quiet, Penny, and take a nap until Mommy wakes up."

"Okay," but I kept my eyes on our mother, just to see if she is going to wink at me to keep her secret that she is really awake and just watching how good we're being.

As we lay there quietly beside our sleeping mommy, the telephone rang out loud from the small living room. Geronimo rushed to answer it, before it woke up the baby and our mommy.

"Hello. Oh, hi, Dad," Geronimo answered. "Because mommy is still sleeping, that's why." Answering all of Daddy's questions as to why he is answering the telephone instead of our mommy, Geronimo laid the telephone down, came back into the bedroom, and shook our mother. "Mommy, wake up, it's Dad on the phone. Mommy, wake up."

"What's the matter, Geronimo? Why won't mommy wake up?" I cried.

Geronimo raced back to the telephone, and I heard him crying into the telephone to our dad. "I don't know, Dad, she just won't wake up, and I shook her really hard."

I can hear the sound of my big brother's voice, and for the first time I could sense he was afraid. My big brother that was never afraid of anything was crying. As he returned to the bedroom, he now seemed so much older to me. He crossed the room to the side of the bed where baby Brandon was lying beside our mother and picked him up and then gently laid him back into his crib. He put his finger to his lip, motioning for us kids to stay quiet. Then he lay down on the other side of our mother, pulling up the covers over all of us, and just starred at me with tears in his eyes. I knew something was terribly wrong when I saw those tears in my big brother's eyes.

We all lay very quietly on the bed with our still sleeping mother until the loud knock on the door. Then many people began pouring into the house with our daddy leading them. The people were in uniforms carrying black bags and pushing a small roller bed that they placed our mother on and then they took her away.

Our mommy never woke up that day. They took her away on that small rolling bed, and she never said goodbye.

V

"When my father and my mother forsake me, then the Lord will take me up. Teach me thy way, O Lord, and lead me in a plain path, because of mine enemies. Deliver me not over unto the will of mine enemies: for false witnesses are risen up against me, and such as breathe out cruelty."
— *Psalms 26:10-12*

Accidental Abandonment

AWAKENED BY THE sudden movement of this woman, my mother, in her hospital bed, I saw that she was having another painful episode from the after-effects of the chemotherapy treatments. I held her hand and waited for the nurse to come in to give her the morphine medication that the doctor has prescribed to help ease the pain. It seemed to take only a couple of minutes for the morphine to calm her pain enough before she drifted back again into her coma-like sleep. Settling back into the old worn recliner in the corner of the hospital room, I too drifted back to sleep, only to recall more memories ...

After my mommy died, our daddy, with the help of his youngest sister, packed up everything we owned into the old station wagon. He moved us to this place in Kansas, to be closer to his mother and father and his oldest sister, who was this woman, my mother-to-be. They would help him with his grief of losing his wife, our mommy, and with the five of us kids.

I was now four years old, Geronimo was five years old, Cassie was three years old, Junio was one year old, and my baby brother Brandon was four weeks old.

Spending only a short time in this place and not finding the kind of the work to support the five of us kids, our daddy decided to move to California. There was another brother living there, and might be able to help him find decent work, and eventually we could all settle out there with him. Therefore, he decided to leave us kids in the care of his family. We were to stay with his family, and he would return for us later, once he settled into a new place. Cassie, being such a crybaby and a daddy's girl, sensed he was about to leave and would not let him out of her sight, so he had to pack up her things and take her with him to California. His youngest sister had begged him to leave Geronimo with her after our mommy died, but he had refused to split any of his children up. Our daddy would not hear of leaving any of us with anyone during that time of his grief.

After being convinced by my grandmother that since he was taking Cassie with him to California anyway, it might be a good idea for Geronimo to stay with his youngest sister and her preacher husband until he returned. Geronimo could be a handful at times, even for Daddy, and needed constant looking after. Besides, his youngest sister had asked for him after our mommy died, and since she and her preacher husband had no children of their own, they would be delighted to have him. They could raise him as their own son in a proper Christian home. My grandmother's admiration for my little brother Junio was enough to convince our daddy to believe that he was doing the right thing by leaving him with her. Our daddy decided that Grandmother and Grandfather should have Junio, and they would raise him in the country in Oklahoma.

Our daddy was determined that he would keep his two girls together and raise them in California with him. He had already asked his oldest sister, this woman, my mother, to take my baby brother Brandon and raise him as her own. He had another favor to ask of her also, which was if she would just keep me until he settled in a new place in California and found work. He promised that he would be back to get me in three months. Reluctantly, this woman, my mother, and her husband both agreed.

Three months seemed like three years to me. That's how long I was to be left with this woman, my mother, and her husband, before my daddy was to return to get me. My daddy left for California with my sister Cassie, and I never saw my daddy again.

There was a terrible car accident on a lonely highway in the middle of the night in the state of Arizona. A semi tractor-trailer truck had jackknifed, hitting an eastern-bound car head on and killing instantly the only occupant in the car driven by my daddy.

My daddy, this woman, my mother's baby brother, had been tragically killed in this accident on his way back to this place in Kansas to get me.

Therefore, I stayed with this woman, my mother, and

her husband, with my four-week-old baby brother Brandon. I knew by the looks they gave me, the quiet tones in their conversation around me, that my grandmother, my daddy's youngest sister and this woman, my mother, felt that it was my fault that my daddy had been killed. That if he had not been driving such a long way from California alone and tired from work, back to this place in Kansas to get me, he would not have died in such a tragic accident.

I cried silently to myself at my daddy's funeral and could only think that my daddy, like my mommy, left me and never said goodbye.

VI

"Behold, how good and pleasant it is for brethren to dwell together in unity!"   *— Psalms 133:1*

Finding Cassie

THERE WAS ONLY one body in the tragic accident that killed my daddy. The driver of the semi tractor-trailer truck had only a few scratches and a bruised shoulder.

There must have been another body. It had to be. Cassie left with my daddy going to California, so she must have been with him on his way back to get me. She was such a crybaby; she would never let him leave her behind. So where was she?

No one knew of my daddy's plans to leave Cassie in California. Let alone with some unknown woman. They had assumed that she too would be coming back with him when he returned to get me.

It was almost two weeks before Cassie was located in the care of a this unknown woman, in the small town in California, close to where my daddy worked, and where he had found a small apartment to live. He had found a nice middle-aged lady that lived in the same apartment complex as he, and had arranged for her to keep Cassie while he was working during the day, and any overtime hours he could get at night. This was the first person that Cassie was comfortable staying with, whenever he had to be gone for any length of time. Therefore, my daddy decided to leave Cassie with this woman to care for her until he returned to this place in Kansas for me.

Watching the news on the television the next evening after our daddy left, this nice middle-aged woman recognized the name of the accident victim from California. She was shocked at the report. Shocked that she knew the accident victim as my daddy, and that his child was with her. She sat frozen in her seat and just stared at Cassie. She kept staring at Cassie while still hearing his name and seeing his face flash across the television screen. She knew this victim, my daddy, was on his way to a place in Kansas to get his oldest daughter that he had left behind. Her heart pulsed hard in her throat as she looked at the bright-eyed, dimple-faced little girl playing quietly in the corner of her living room. She silently wept to herself for him and this child's unknown loss of yet another parent. Wiping her eyes, she went to my sister, bent over her and kissed her forehead. Cassie smiled up at the nice woman and showed her the dolly she was playing with and continued with her enjoyment of playing house with her dolly, oblivious of the moisture in the woman's eyes.

My father had given this woman an emergency telephone number at the time of his departure, that she must find. Locating the telephone number, she made the call to my grandmother and told her about the news report she had heard, and that Cassie was in her care. Briefly exchanging information and giving my grandmother directions to her home, it was arranged that my uncle, who lived only two hours away in another town in California, would pick Cassie up, and bring her back to Oklahoma.

My sister was to live with my grandmother and grandfather and my other brother Junio in the country in Oklahoma.

VII

"And it came to pass in those days, that he went out into a mountain to pray, and continued all night in prayer to God." — *St. Luke 6:12*

Decisions of Life

THE DECISION WAS made by my grandmother and my daddy's youngest sister who lived in Colorado, as to where I would be living and with whom. Since I was already at this woman, my mother, and her husband's house, it made sense that I should remain there to live with them, and my baby brother Brandon.

Grandmother's oldest daughter was always excluded from any discussions on decisions that were made, including this one. It did not matter if the decisions were of major significance or of minor insignificance, not even if they affected her. My grandmother always called upon her youngest daughter, who was married to a preacher, for her opinion on everything. Whether it involved other members of their family, or which store she should shop at, to what doctor she should see. However, it was the oldest daughter, along with her husband, who did all the necessary comings and goings that had to be done for my grandmother and grandfather. Still, Grandmother would always have to consult her youngest daughter, for her opinion and advice on anything first.

All I know and remember is that our daddy's intentions were to keep and raise his two girls together, with him. Didn't my daddy's wishes for his two girls mean anything to them? I would have preferred to be with my big brother Geronimo, but I did not like my grandmother's youngest daughter. Not even when we lived in Colorado, before our mommy died. My grandmother's youngest daughter did not like my mommy very much, and she did not like me either. I guess, because I looked too much like my mommy. All I ever heard out of her mouth was, "Penny looks just like her mother, and even acts like her, too." Then she would find some reason to fuss at me. However, she did like my big brother Geronimo for some reason. Everyone always said he was bad and acted like a little savage Indian. I guess that was how he got his nickname. Still, she adored him and always brought him little gifts of toys, clothes and candy whenever she came to visit us. She never brought me gifts, or candy, or clothes, or anything else. My mommy recognized the difference she was making between her children, often chastising her about this treatment and telling her that she preferred that she did not spoil Geronimo so much. Nevertheless, my daddy's youngest sister would just ignore her and do as she pleased without regard to my mother or to me. My big brother Geronimo always shared his gifts of toys and candy that she bought to him with me after she left our home.

My daddy's youngest sister also loved my Uncle Arthur's little lying kids a lot. They were so properly raised and all — the same cousins who always seemed to get my big brother and me into trouble whenever we visited their house. And sometimes the razor strap for Geronimo as his punishment.

My grandmother and my daddy's youngest sister had made the decision for their son and brother's five children. My big brother Geronimo, who was five years old, would remain with and live in Colorado at my daddy's youngest sister and her preacher husband's home. My sister Cassie, who was three years old, and other brother Junio, who was one year old, would remain with and live in the country in Oklahoma at my grandmother and grandfather's home. My baby brother Brandon, who was four weeks old, would remain with and live in Kansas at my daddy's oldest sister and her alcoholic husband's home. Then there was me, who had already been the topic of concerned discussion earlier by my grandmother and her youngest daughter, was to remain where I had been left.

I swore to myself that I would never forgive my grandmother or my daddy's youngest sister for making such a decision about my life without asking me first. They never asked me what I wanted or where I wanted to live. However, what practical decision could I make at four years old? Whom did I know to ask for to say where I wanted to go live? I knew no one but these people, my daddy's family. I didn't know any of my mommy's family, and no one ever mentioned them. All I knew or heard about my mother's family was that they lived somewhere called Indianapolis, Indiana. I knew I had another grandmother, which was my mommy's mother, whom they would talk about, called Grandma Byrde. I didn't know or remember her. I did, however, have enough sense at four years old to know that I did not want to be here in this place in

Kansas, with this woman, my mother, and her alcoholic husband.

They did not love me, and they did not want me there any more than I wanted to be there with them. I was too much like my mommy, whom they all must have hated, by the things they said about her. I was a four-year-old burden and needed to be cared for by someone. My daddy's youngest sister would say "they did not believe in throwing away any of their children. We do what we can, the best we can, and that's all we can do" was the phrase she often used. Therefore, I became an unwanted obligation and burden to them all.

Looking as if I could be the twin of my mommy was a daily reminder to everyone that had known her. I had no facial features that resembled my daddy, or any of my brothers and sister. I looked my mommy. I was darker in complexion, with a long ski-sloped nose, high cheekbones and a head full of thick, coal black, very coarse, nappy hair. My sister's hair was thin, short, reddish brown and fine like cotton. My sister and brothers all looked alike and resembled my daddy and his family in some kind of way.

This woman, my mother, would wash, comb and brush, then press and braid my coarse, nappy hair. Then everyone would say that I looked like an evil little black Indian girl. Sometimes while getting my hair done, I was hit over the head several times with the brush if I didn't sit still, or would get a whipping with the switches if I cried when it hurt. It was rough sitting there quietly while she combed through my thick, coarse, nappy hair. I wished that my hair would be like my sister's then. I learned quickly how to hold my breath, and would close my eyes when that hot, pressing comb would come close to frying my ears and burning the kitchen edges of my neck. This woman, my mother, would keep the pressing comb on the blue flames of the stove so long that the hair grease sizzled like fish frying in a pan of hot oil, as she pulled the hot iron comb through my hair.

I did look liked a little black Indian with evil eyes, once she had finished. My eyes were bloodshot from holding back tears while the hair ritual was being performed with fire and a hot iron on my head. That is when I would think of my big brother Geronimo. He was the one given the Indian nickname, but I was the one who looked like an Indian, with evil eyes, and like my mommy.

My life as I had known it before with my daddy and mommy was no more. It began again at age four years old, in this place in Kansas, living with this woman, my mother, her alcoholic husband, and my baby brother, Brandon.

VIII

"For thou has been strength to the poor, a strength to the needy in his distress, a refuge from the storm, a shadow from the heat, when the blast of the terrible ones is as strong against the wall."   — *Isaiah 25:4*

Weathering the Storms

THE SUN WAS beginning to set when my youngest daughter, Melanie, awakened me. She arrived just before visiting hours were over and had come to the hospital to sit with the only grandmother she has known, this woman, my mother. Retrieving a blanket from the small linen closet in the bathroom of the hospital room, she lightly kissed her grandmother, then pulled a chair up close by me. We talked quietly about how comfortable her grandmother appears, as she is sleeping peacefully on the hospital bed. I did not tell her that the peaceful comfort is from the help of morphine injections that have been administered by the nurse.

This woman, my mother, who lay there looking so peaceful and comfortable while she slept was weathering a storm.

She lay there quietly and uncomplaining, while weathering a storm with the death-sentence disease that was ravishing her body and tossing her insides with such a force, that made death a glad welcoming.

Tears burned my eyes, but not wanting Melanie to see me cry, I left for a short walk down the hospital corridor. I was back in less than five minutes for fear of not being there if this woman, my mother, should awaken and need me. I did not want to miss any time that I have left with her. Relieved and feeling comfortable that she is still sleeping, I returned to my corner. Not wanting to drift back to sleep, I sat up straight in the old recliner, and tried to read a magazine left in the hospital room by another visitor. Looking, but not seeing the words or the pictures in the magazine, my mind and concentration was on other flashes of pictures from violent storms. Wide awake and not dreaming, the recall of memories still came flooding back. Playing other storms that this woman, my mother, had weathered many times through in the past.

The drinking, arguing and the fighting would on go for hours. Sometimes I felt sorry for this woman, my mother, but sometimes I did not. I think, because I thought she was so mean to me all the time. It seemed that I got a whipping all the time, for everything, and for nothing. For my making too much noise either when I played with my dolly, or not making up my bed the right way. Like a kid knows how to make a bed with perfect corners, and fluff the pillows correctly.

It was my job every morning to take out the pee jar that sat behind my bedroom door. There was no running water in the kitchen and no bathroom in this small, four-roomed house. We had to go in a pee jar during the night. A pee jar that had to be in my bedroom that everyone used. Sometimes I would forget to take the overnight pee and other collections in the jar to the old outhouse that sat near the alley to dump. Why I got a whipping for not remembering to take out everyone else's pee was beyond me. Why the pee jar had to sit in my bedroom was way beyond me, especially since they had to come into my bedroom to use it. I did not understand it, but I hated it, and hated them.

So therefore, my reasoning for not caring about them fighting all the time, or her being hurt by her husband was not my concern. At least when he was beating her, she was not beating me. She was hurting me all the time with those braided switches, or that brown electrical extension cord, that left those bloody welts all over my body. I felt like one of those child slaves in the movies that I saw on our black and white television. Their masters were always whipping the slaves when they disobeyed, did not do their chores or tried to run away. That is how I felt, like a slave, thinking about running away to the Promised Land. After the first whipping with the extension cord, seeing my bloody legs and feeling the sting of the pain rippling from the welts, I thought I would probably never walk again. That is when I began to hate this woman, my mother, and wished I were dead like my mommy.

The welts healed, and I forgot about the whippings and tried to remember all my chores and to be a good girl so as not to get another one. Massaging my wounds, I wondered why this woman, my mother, let her husband beat her. I never had the courage to ask for fear she would take her anger out on me, until one day after a terrible beating occurred. Her drunken husband had tired himself from beating her, he left in the car to go carousing for a while. I begged her to take my baby brother and me and just leave while he was gone. She refused and just yelled at me. I asked her why we couldn't just go to Grandmother's house in the country in Oklahoma, so she wouldn't have to let him do this to her, and then I wished that I hadn't asked.

It was because of me was all that was said.

This woman, my mother, cleaned her cuts and bruises, and took my crying baby brother Brandon with her into her bedroom to rest, before he came back. She never told me to come with her, or even allowed me in the bedroom. She yelled at me, told me it was my fault, and that things would be a lot better if I was not there. I never asked her again, or wanted to be with her and my baby brother Brandon during these times. I stayed in my bedroom in the back of the house, thinking of my mommy, and hated this woman, my mother, even more.

It was my fault that her husband beat her all the time. Her husband beat her because he was pressured into having to take me in and care for me, along with my baby brother Brandon. A decision he had not been asked about or involved in. A decision that she had allowed her mother and, as he put it, her "sanctified preacher's wife sister," to make for her. I could tell that by the names he called this woman, my mother, her sister and my grandmother, that he did not think much of these women at all.

Neither one of them wanted me. He didn't mind the baby, but another child, one that he was not given a choice on. His excuse was that he could not afford to take care of two kids that did not belong to him with the salary he made. It was not that he could not afford to take care of us. It was because he didn't get a choice. Although this woman, my mother, hated girls, he fell in love with Cassie, and would have loved to have had her instead. If he had to take in any of the five children he would have preferred to have my sister Cassie, and had told this to everyone. He thought she was so adorable with those dimples and that cute smile of hers. However, the decision had already been discussed and made. It was up to our grandmother who had somehow legally appointed herself as our guardian. It was up to her; there would not be any more discussion as to where which child would live, and with whom. So that was that, and no questions to be asked.

Still I wondered about all the fights and arguments, and if it could be my fault, so I started to listen whenever they began to get loud. I was trying to hear my name, to find out what I did to cause the fights. But I never heard her husband mention my name when they fought. I did hear the mean things he would say about their own child — a son who had left home at eighteen years of age for the armed services, and then went on to live out on the West Coast. A son that he obviously hated.

Her husband would drink corn liquor and bottles of Schlitz beer all day long and then start horrible fights with this woman, my mother. Afterward, seeing her face all bloody, her eyes swollen shut and her lips split open, I cried quietly to myself for her. The fear of losing her, and the thought of her dying from those beatings washed over me, that I would once again be left alone without another mother.

She would try desperately to hide the bruises and black eyes from everyone and from him the next day, for fear that he would accuse her of causing him to do such things to her. She didn't have to tell or hide the bruises from anyone anyway; everyone already knew what was happening to her.

Listening even more to those arguments, I soon put things together as to why he beat her. The fights were about her and her family, but mostly about their son. The son that he obviously hated so much, and said that he did not resemble him in any way. It was kind of like me with my daddy, and how I looked exactly like my mommy that there was nothing left of my body features to show off my daddy. His son looked almost exactly like his mother and had nothing left to show off his father. This woman, my mother's husband, swore that the child was not and could not possibly be his. They had only dated for a short while before she told him that she was pregnant. It did not matter, he still had to marry her. Her father and her husband's stepfather, who happened to be her father's brother, insisted that it was the right thing to do. An arranged marriage without love, and a child on the way took place shortly thereafter.

Nevertheless, when this woman, my mother, lashed out at me after the arguments and fights with him, I knew it was because she could not do so with him. I even understood a little now why she said it was because of me. I, like her son, was a constant reminder of the fathers that we did or did not look like. No matter how awful he was to her, he was considered a good man, so no one ever helped her or tried to stop him. Not even the police, when 911 emergency calls were made. He had worked for the city for too many years for them to lose a good worker. He went to work every night, was never late, never took any sick days or vacation time off, kept a roof over her head, and she never had to work a day in her life, outside of the house. So what was her problem, what could she do or say to anyone about anything?

Not only did they continue to fight among themselves, they also fought about and with other family members. Particularly with my Uncle Fletcher, who was this woman, my mother's younger brother. He and his girlfriend would come over to our house on Saturday nights to join in with the drinking and so-called socializing. Now Uncle Fletcher was considered to be a ladies' man, had a wife and six children of his own, but always had plenty of other women on the side and a different one every time he came to our house.

He always found a reason to chastise me for something every time he came to our house. I could tell by the way he talked about me, how I looked and acted so much like *"...that damn Joan,"* as he put it, that he didn't care for my mommy very much. Something was said or done a long time ago, in Michigan where we all once lived before moving to Colorado, between my mommy, daddy, Uncle Fletcher and his wife, and my daddy's meddling youngest sister, that made everyone hate my mommy. I do not know, or understand yet what it was all about, but I hated him anyway for talking about my mommy. I would roll evil-looking eyes at him whenever he made these comments about my mommy, but about me. If he caught me doing this, he would make me kneel in a corner with my face to the wall for at least an hour. This was his special punishment he liked to use for all his nieces and nephews, especially when he was drinking, and had one of his women with him. Funny thing is, he never bothered about punishing his own children. Half of the time he never even knew where or what his children were doing. His children all ran the streets, at all hours of the day and night, and got into trouble all the time, even the youngest one, who was only five years old. He had no control over them, or his own house. However, he could sure come into someone else's house and discipline their children.

After about forty-five minutes with my nose stuck in the corner of the wall, knees aching and numb from the blood standing in huddled pouches of my calves, this woman, my mother's drunk husband, frowned at my Uncle Fletcher, then told me to get up and go to my bedroom. I was so surprised that in his drunkenness, that he had even paid any attention as to what was going on between my uncle and me.

He was drunk, but he was also listening, watching everything, and getting mad as hell at my uncle. Uncle Fletcher, who was his brother-in-law, had the nerve to come into his house, chastise his little unwanted orphaned child, and never bothered to even know where his own children were or what they were doing. Never mind the fact that he had brought another woman that wasn't his wife into his home. This woman, my mother's drunk husband told my uncle just what he thought about him and told him to leave. Uncle Fletcher refused, saying he could come and visit his sister at her house whenever he got good and damn ready. And the argument started. And it grew louder and nastier by the minute. This woman, my mother, tried to stop them, but it was no use. She tried to make my uncle shut up and leave when her husband went into their bedroom, but it was too late. He had gone to retrieve his old hunting rifle. Determined to prove that he was the man of his house, he first aimed the rifle at Uncle Fletcher, then at everyone in the room, then shot the rifle straight up into the ceiling of the house. He cussed at my uncle to leave, and to take his whore with him. But Uncle Fletcher, not wanting to be outdone in front of his woman, went outside, opened the trunk of his pink and black Buick Roadmaster Special, and pulled out his 4-10 shotgun.

He did not come back to the house; he called out to his sister's husband, pointed to his car, a white Chevrolet Bel-Air, then proceeded to break all the windows in the car with the butt of the rifle. This woman, my mother, was on the telephone calling the police, but her husband was already out the door with his old hunting rifle. He, like my uncle, took the butt of his rifle and began breaking the windows, the lights and the mirrors on my uncle's car. Uncle Fletcher was enraged and had loaded his 4-10 shotgun and was ready to aim when the police siren stopped him.

Neither of them was arrested, ticketed or punished for their actions that night. This woman, my mother's husband, who worked for the city, explained to the police officers that things had gotten a little out of hand, and that it was all just a misunderstanding between them. I, however, was punished again that same night, after everyone had left, by this woman, my mother. It was my fault that the argument happened, and that the fight had started, and now more money was to be spent to fix the broken windows in the car. And her husband beat her afterwards.

For years, she continually endured the beatings and the verbal abuse from this upstanding man of the community. This man, her husband, that gave to everyone. All the kids in town adored him, everyone came to borrow from him, and everyone came to visit him. Everyone loved him, and he loved everyone, except his own wife and child, and me.

She survived his beatings, and I survived her whippings.

IX

"He sitteth in the lurking places of the villages: in the se-cret places doth he murder the innocent: his eyes are priv-ily set against the poor. He lieth in wait secretly as a lion in his den: he lieth in wait to catch the poor: he doth catch the poor, when he draweth him into his net. He croucheth, and humbleth himself, that the poor may fall by his strong ones."   — *Psalms 10:8-10*

Hushed Nightmares

I FELT MY insides were exploding out through my mouth, as the large hand pressed against my face and his body smashed down on mine. No sound could come out of my mouth between the nasty tasting fingers, but I could hear myself screaming in my ears as the burning tears rolled down the side of my head. Before finishing his romp and rolling from atop of my limp five-year-old body, he kept his hand over my mouth, and then whis-pered in my ear. All that I remembered then was a simi-lar secret from long ago, and I vowed again not to tell anyone. There was no one to tell. My big brother Geronimo was far away and living in his own hell with my daddy's youngest sister and her preacher husband.

My eyes swollen and red from trying to hold the tears back, I made another vow to myself that I would not cry any more. At least, not let anyone see or hear me cry. I learned to cry inside to myself, without shedding the burning tears to show that I hurt.

He was the son of one of my daddy's brothers. Whenever he was in town, he always came knocking at the door late at night. This woman, my mother, would let him stay at our house when her husband left for work, as long as he was up and out before her husband came back home in the morning. She allowed him to sleep in my bedroom, in my bed with me, as long as he was quiet and didn't wake me. He was quiet, she never heard him, but he did wake me. I did not tell, I did not cry, I hated him, I hated everything, and especially her for letting him hurt me. Hurting me worse than any of the whippings I received from her. I wished even harder that I were dead.

I began to hate my mommy now, for leaving me. Not just for leaving me, but for leaving my big brother Geronimo, too. I was not worried about the others; they were all loved and adored by everyone. That's because they were younger and didn't understand or remember our mommy and daddy. They adapted to their new surroundings very easily without questions, and happily accepted the love they received. They did not know the cruel, insane and abusive fate that had been cast upon their older brother and sister.

Summer vacation and holidays were the only times my big brother Geronimo came to visit, along with daddy's youngest sister. The look in his eyes told me that he was living and playing a familiar role. The same role as I was living and playing. Although my daddy's youngest sister seemed to adore him, she and her preacher husband whipped him unmercifully for everything that he did. However, they didn't whip him at the time of the incidents when he did these bad things. They would wait until the end of the week and keep tally of everything he did. Her preacher husband would collect switches and store them in the corner of the closet each day when he arrived home from work. Some days he would even have my big brother Geronimo collect the switches that were to be used for his punishment. Daily reminders of what was to come on Saturday morning faced him each time he opened that closet door to hang up his jacket. And my big brother Geronimo began to hate as I did. He too began to hate everyone and everything that surrounded him. He didn't care any more either, and began to be defiant at home, at school, and caused trouble everywhere that he went. He knew that he was going to get a whipping anyway at the end of the week, so why not do something that was deserving of the beating to come.

He still played with matches a lot, and when he was five and a half years old, he set a car on fire. It was also rumored that he was the one who set fire to the principal's office at his school. Soon afterward, he changed to another school, although never formerly accused of setting the fire. He had also started stealing things. They were small, inexpensive items at first. Later, he was bolder with his stealing, and the items were more expensive. He received an allowance weekly, but he chose to save his money for the day he would need it most. The day that he planned to run away from the home that my daddy's youngest sister and her preacher husband had provided for him.

On those occasions when my big brother Geronimo came to visit, we did not play together as we used to do;

we did not share toys or candy. We did not need to. We had grown past those childish things, and now only shared unspoken words. An unspoken word of silence, exchanged only through eye contact, was the conversation between my big brother and me. Eyes that have been called evil looking. Eyes that spoke the words that we dared not say aloud. Eyes that cried without tears, that said to each other I know your pain is the same as mine. Vacant eyes reflecting as if looking in a mirror showing a pain so deep inside each of us, that only we could see and feel. We shared the pain of separation. The pain of how dramatically our life changed in such a short period since our mommy's death. We felt each other's pain from the life that had been chosen for the two us. A moistened blink from both of our eyes, and he, like me, thinking of our mommy, we both turned our heads away for an instant, then quickly back to each other. Smiling now as we both think of her, he took my hand in his and squeezed it as a vow to always love me. Our silent conversation had ended, and we ran off to join the others.

Overhearing conversations between my daddy's two sisters made me realize just how much my big brother and I were disciplined, and so differently from the others. At the end of the week, the switches that had been collected in the closet were used separately or sometimes braided together as a whip on my big brother. My daddy's youngest sister's preacher husband would make my big brother lie across his bed, naked, and beat him until all the switches were broken in shreds, or until he got tired. Sometimes he would rest awhile and continue to beat him some more. Other times he would take him out to the garage behind their house, close the door and beat him for all the things that he had done during the week. They laughed about this, as if talking about flowers in the garden, while my daddy's youngest sister sipped on her peppermint schnapps from the bottle hidden in her purse, and this woman, my mother, drank Schlitz beer from a paper towel-wrapped glass. I hated them both.

I hated my daddy's youngest sister even more, for being such a hypocrite and pretending to love my big brother so much when my mommy died. She only pretended to want him because she never had any children of her own, except for one, a little boy. He had died prematurely, and she and her preacher husband never had any more. She was just jealous of my mommy having three boys and two girls, so she pretended to love my big brother, and did things for him that she would have done for her own son if he had lived.

Vacation time was nearly over, and my big brother would go away, back home to Colorado with my daddy's youngest sister and her preacher husband. I didn't know when I would see him again, but I would always remember the quiet time we spent together. And I cried inside for him now, even before he left, because I knew of the quiet storms he, like I, would have to continue to weather before the calm would come.

X

"For God shall bring every work into judgment, with every secret thing. — *Ecclesiastes 12:14*

Family Portraits

THERE WERE ALWAYS pictures taken on arrival and departure of family, whenever they came to visit. Usually these pictures were taken in the front of my grandmother's house in the country, in Oklahoma. There were pictures of my daddy's sisters and his brothers. Then pictures of all his brothers and sisters posing with my grandmother and grandfather together. Of course, there were tons of pictures of my entire grandmother's many grandchildren, and some great grandchildren. Either together, or caught at a special moment during their play.

Over the years of picture-taking by family members and friends, there amounted quite a collection for the many family albums. Pictures of family gatherings, party snapshots and special occasions, spilled over in shoeboxes, hatboxes and old unused dresser drawers.

There were pictures of my dad, young and old. There were pictures of him posing with friends when he was in the army. There were pictures of him with some of his old girlfriends. There were pictures of his brothers and sisters with their old and new friends. There were pictures of this woman, my mother, and my daddy riding on an old bicycle. There were pictures of four men looking like bank robbers out of an old Western picture. There was a picture of an old red-haired Irishman with a long moustache, which was my grandmother's father. Even pictures of my daddy with his pet pig.

Out of all those pictures in those boxes of my father's family, I found none of him with his wife, my mommy. Not a picture of him with the five of us kids. You would think that after five children there would be at least one picture of all of us as a family, or something. I went through all those pictures to try to find a picture of my mommy. However, there was none found in any of the boxes. There were several of my other uncles with their wives. There was a picture of my daddy's youngest sisters sitting on the lap of a man showing her sweetheart tattoo on her arm. The tattoo had the same name as her preacher husband, but the man was not her husband.

I needed to see a picture of my mommy. Everyone says that I am the spitting image of her, but I cannot see it because I don't know what she looks like. I look in the mirror each day and try to remember her face. If only I could just see her face in the mirror and look into her eyes through mine, then maybe I could see what it was that everyone saw in her face that they didn't like. I stared at the mirror until my eyes started to burn with the tears that I dared not shed, and wondered if her eyes are also burning with the same kind of tears. I remembered my mommy, lying on the bed with one eye open and one eye closed, watching us, yet asleep. That is the only picture that I have of my mommy.

A picture that will never be processed on film for anyone else to see. A picture that will never be shared with other loved ones. I have a picture of my mommy that will forever be buried in my mind.

XI

"Thou art my hiding place and my shield: I hope in thy word."   — *Psalms 119:114*

Moving Day

As I LOOKED around my bedroom one last time, I walked back into the small kitchen; I let out a silent sigh of relief. I thanked God for finally starting on His crusade to rescue me. Another quick glance back into my bedroom, while adjusting the shoulder strap for more comfort, I thought of the painful nightmares that were real, and I prayed now that I could finally rid myself of them. Rid myself of the painful nightmares and of the thoughts I had that somehow they were punishment from this woman, my mother. The sick punishment that she had to have witnessed through the small open hole in the back of my closet.

While packing my belongings into boxes, I found an open hole in the wall of my closet, covered by an old dusty curtain. An open hole that I never knew was there, but she must have known it was there. It was her house. It had been her house long before I had ever moved there to live with her. An open hole looked straight into this woman, my mother's bedroom from my bedroom. It was an open hole that I know this woman, my mother, had to have seen what had been done to me. An open hole that proved even more to me how much this woman, my mother, hated me.

"Penny, hurry up and finish packing those boxes, it's time to go," this woman, my mother, yelled.

"Yes, ma'am," I answered. I sighed once more, and continued packing my belongings into the boxes and bags as fast as I could, forgetting the open hole. . Wincing from the pain in my shoulder, I sat down for only a minute, until the pain eased away. Playing outside with the next door neighbors kids one day, clumsy me tripped and fell on a large dog bone laying in the yard. The sound of my bone cracking as it hit the dog bone was that of a dry limb from a tree. It hurt and I wanted to cry, but didn't, and I didn't tell for fear of getting into trouble. My collarbone was broken, started mending back together, yet crooked, before this woman, my mother, noticed that something was wrong with me. I walked around bent over for four days before she finally took me to the doctor. Just another of her hatred punishment, I thought she had for me.

God, I hated her and the sound of her voice. Always yelling, and so mean acting towards me. I wish I were dead sometimes just so I could not hear her voice. Continuing to check all the dresser drawers, I ignored the closet and checked under my bed one more time. Just to make sure nothing was underneath it before the bed was ready to move. Finishing in the bedroom, I went into the kitchen to help pack the dishes. The sooner I could help finish, the sooner we'd be out this four-room box called a house. At least, the new house would have a toilet inside the house, thank God.

This should be a happy moment for most families that are moving into a new or bigger house. We were not like most families I realized early on in coming to live here. There was never any happiness around here. At least, none that I had seen, unless you count the drinking and the fighting that went on. We were moving now, so maybe we could find happiness in the new place.

At last, no more going outside in the middle of the night to use that funky outhouse that sat by the alley. No more of having to wash out dirty old funky piss jars that were used in the privacy of my bedroom, behind closed doors. This woman, my mother never watched over me when I had to go to that funky outhouse that sat by the alley in the middle of night. That funky outhouse that many strangers in the night took liberty of using as a public bathroom.

I learned by the age of six, however, how to hold my pee overnight. I decided I would rather have a stomach-ache the next morning from holding my pee, than to have to go to that funky outhouse in the middle of the night. Some mornings it felt as if my stomach was ready to ex-plode from holding my pee all night. That is what I did, until we finally moved.

We were moving into a bigger house that had a toilet and a face bowl inside the house, with a kitchen that had running water, and built in sinks, three bedrooms, and a big living room. That was going to be happiness enough for me. Thank you, God.

XII

"Though I walk in the midst of trouble, thou wilt revive me." — *Psalms 138:7*

New Beginnings

MOVING INTO THIS new and bigger house soon proved to be no different from the old, small four-room house. There was still no love or happiness, no hugs or kisses; anger and hatred seemed to be the only emotions allowed to fill the rooms. Laughter seemed acceptable only if the old black and white television set was playing. The years passed on, and everything remained the same, except for one thing.

I was older now. Old enough to walk to the store by myself and buy the spirited liquids they each loved so much. I had to walk to the liquor store, or the little grocery store down the street to buy the beer and liquor for them, when they were both too drunk to drive. Their drinking seemed to be a daily, non-stop routine, starting at noon and ending late into the night. I think drinking was the only thing they loved together, until the fights started.

Imagine now, me, a young child allowed to purchase alcoholic beverages like an adult. It was so humiliating, I hated them for making me do this, and the storeowners for selling it to me, as if it was okay. The storeowners knew them both well, and thought of her husband as being good people, so I never was turned away or shooed from the store because of my age. Me, the little orphan kid belonging to the people the storeowners knew so well. I came to their store, with money and a note tied in a handkerchief. The storeowners eagerly packaged up the contents on the list, after removing the money, and handed over to me a brown paper sack. A sack heavy from bottles of Schlitz beer, Tareyton and no filtered Camel cigarettes, and sometimes a bottle of corn liquor. And because I was such a polite little black girl, there would be a special surprise of a candy bar or stale bubble gum for me. God, I hated it, and was so embarrassed that the candy didn't matter. I didn't want any of it. What I hated even more were the stares I got from other patrons in the store. Then having to walk home, past the houses of kids that I went to school with, and they knowing what I had in the brown paper sacks. I was starting to become embarrassed of myself, of who I was and what I was.

At the age of nine years old, I was alone, unhappy, unloved, and now embarrassed. I wished and prayed to God that I would die. I figured that the best way to remedy my embarrassment and my living situation with these people was to die. I prayed to God if He would just send me back to my real mommy and daddy, and I dreamed of dying each night. I wanted to be as far away from this place that I knew could only be hell or even worse. I thought death was my only answer, but God was not listening to my prayers. I guess God wanted me to suffer a little longer; maybe He did not like me either. I stopped praying to Him for death, and starting thinking of my brothers and sister, and knew that I needed to live for them. Just in case, they might need me some day, later in life. Besides, I did not want to piss this woman, my mother, off and have her start whipping my baby brother Brandon, because I was not around any more. Although I did not feel close to my sister and brother who lived with my grandmother, I felt that I might need to be around for them later. I did not worry so much about my big brother Geronimo, who was so far away in Colorado, going through his sordid hell. He had always been a strong and smart one and would know how to take care of himself. I decided to live and show them all that they would not and could not beat me down. I would live and get the hell out of this place and go as far a way as possible, as soon as I reached the age of eighteen years old. I only had nine more years to go.

School was my refuge. I loved school and my teachers, and liked some of the kids in my class. Most of all, I loved the books and poems, and even did some writing of my own. At recess, instead of playing on the swings or ball with the other kids, I found a quiet corner to read. I read everything that I could get my hands. Reading books was something I could do that did not seem to bother this woman, my mother. Whenever I was not playing with my baby brother Brandon or doing my chores, I stayed in my bedroom and read, wrote my own poems and hid them away in my closet before leaving my room. I even read the Bible through two times, and that was really hard to read because of some of the words and names of all the old prophets, but I understood most of it. Some of it even seemed to apply to me, especially the book of *Psalms* when David cried out to the Lord for mercy, and then gave thanks and praises even before God blessed him.

My baby brother Brandon was getting older and becoming a real momma's boy. After all, this was the only mother he has ever known. And she loved and adored him, especially since he called her Mommy, unlike me, I called her nothing. I simply answered when spoken to and asked her for whatever I needed without having to use a name, and I called her husband by his first name when responding to him. I knew it just pissed this woman, my mother, off that I would not call her mom, or mommy like my little brother. This woman, my mother, was my daddy's oldest sister, which makes her my *aunt,* and not my *mother.* All of her other nieces and nephews and other kids in the neighborhood call her Aunt Johnnie and call her husband Uncle Ben. I refuse to call her that, too.

Her real name is JohnSella, so I decided that I would call her "J'sol" for a nickname, one that is all my own. I put lots of emphasis on the "J" when I say it. She did not like it at all. I thought it was a great name. At least, I was calling her something.

It was a start, a new beginning in a way, for J'sol and me.

XIII

"Be not far from me; for trouble is near; for there is none to help." — *Psalms 22:11*

A New Life

LEARNING AT AN early age in life how to keep secrets, one more secret shared with my best friend shouldn't be too hard to keep. A secret that I had to keep from J'sol and the rest of my family. Although my best friend would beg me daily to tell J'sol, I still refused. I had not gotten a whipping for a long time now, and I was not going to give her reason to start again. My best friend knew how J'sol was and understood why I could not tell. But she was concerned about my not receiving the proper attention that I should be getting. But she kept my secret. She was the best friend that anyone could have in their life, and mine for sure right now. We became friends almost instantly when she and her huge family moved across the street from us. I truly believe that she was my angel sent by God as my earthly protector. She became my confidant of solace, and I trusted her with everything. Oh, she scolded me sometimes whenever I'd say or do something negative, or jump to conclusions about people. She even helped me to deal with my family and the hate that I had built up through the years. Of course, I never went into the details of why I hated them so much with her, but she could feel my pain. That's how close we had become. She was like a big sister that I never had, so I didn't mind her scolding me. She loved me just as much as her other sisters. Boy, did she have a lot of sisters and brothers, twelve of them all together. *"Rep,"* her father, a Baptist minister, was a good and fine upstanding man in the church and the community. He was a loving man to his wife and children. Her mother *"Ruby,"* was a strong and robust, loving woman. I spent as much time as allowed by J'sol with her and her family. They were a real family, and I wanted to be as much a part of it as possible. And I thanked God once again for sending them to me.

My best friend and I knew that if J'sol found out that I was pregnant that she probably would have beaten the baby out of me. My plan was to leave as soon as I finished high school, go straight to California, and not tell anyone, except for my best friend, where I was. She never even suspected anything, let alone noticed my changing body size, or heard me heaving in the bathroom every morning. That is how much attention J'sol paid to me. Just like when I broke my collarbone. There was no way I was going to tell her or anyone else in this family. Eventually, it was out, all seven and a half months of my baby and me. J'sol caught a glimpse of me as I walked through the front door, and I heard her gasp. A gasp that sounded as a balloon does when the air has suddenly escaped from its rubber form. I stopped dead in my tracks as she pointed toward her bedroom. Her bedroom, not mine. Her bedroom, that she never asked me to come along before when she and my baby brother Brandon sought shelter and rest after her beatings. Her bedroom, that for years, I cried inside of myself to follow her. Her bedroom, that she now ordered me into. I didn't give her the chance to even ask what she was already suspicious of. I just blurted it out to save her the obvious pain that was showing on her face. I wasn't in trouble, like I thought, just banished to my bedroom, until she decided what to do with me. I was not whipped or beaten as expected. I thought of trying several dumb ways of killing myself while waiting in my bedroom— but stopped when I thought of my dying and my baby living, and then having to live here with them.

J'sol did as I expected she would, called my grandmother. And, of course, my grandmother immediately called her youngest daughter. I refused to tell J'sol and my grandmother who the father was. Why should I tell them? They had no idea who or what he was, and I was not about to tell them, so they could do God only knows what to him. I had met him at school one day while waiting for the last bell to ring for class. He was taking a break from his construction work at the school. As he passed by, he whistled at me. I just ignored him at first, but every day after that he would always seem to be wherever I went. And he'd whistle, then flash that bright smile of his at me. He finally came up to me and asked me to join him for lunch one day. Hesitant at first, but I thought what harm could come from lunch on the school grounds; besides my girlfriend was always close by. Every day after that first lunch, he would be waiting for me outside my school, with lunch in hand. We soon became very close friends, and I fell madly in love him. He was fun to talk to and was always a perfect gentleman with me.

So calling my grandmother didn't matter to me. She did not love me, and she knew that I knew it, and that I did not care and had no intention of telling her anything about him. She was just my legal guardian, and only accepted me since I was her son's child. Besides, she was getting regular social security checks for all of us kids. However, she only had two of my siblings. She also thought and said that I looked too much like my mommy, and thought I had such an attitude about me. I never liked going to visit at my grandmother's house, like most kids. I seemed to get into trouble whenever I was out there and got a whipping with the elm switches. The other kids may have been the culprit, but because I was the oldest, that made me responsible. Grandmother, like her youngest daughter, made big differences among us children. Whether it was from the gifts that she bought for us, or the comments she would make.

One comment from my grandmother that still sticks in my mind with pain was when, as young children, we would ask what she thought we would be when we grew up. She responded so lovingly to everyone, except me. To my brother Junio, she said, "My baby boy is going to be a doctor or an engineer"; to Brandon she said, "You are so smart, you could be an architect or a scientist." Then to my sister Cassie she said, "My little princess going to marry an attorney one day and be his secretary." Changing her loving expression shown toward them, she looked at me and with a slight wave of her hand said, "Oh, Penny, she is probably going to be just another street walker. Who knows with her?" I cried inside to myself. I knew how she truly felt about me then. Hatred. I did not care, because I hated her, too.

The following week grandmother's youngest daughter came home to decide with her what was to be done about my dilemma. Again, she did not include her oldest daughter in any decisions to be made. They decided between the two of them, that I should give the baby I was carrying to the youngest daughter to raise as her own. I thought that they must be out of their minds, or drunk with confusion if they thought that I was going to let that woman or any of them in this family have my child. I would kill myself for real.

I graduated from high school with good grades, in the top twenty-five percent of my class of 240 students, and I was seven months pregnant. Not telling anyone except my best friend that I was pregnant kept me from getting the prenatal care usually done in the first few months of pregnancy. Surprisingly, I was in excellent health, and delivered an 8.4-pound baby girl in the scorching hot month of August. She was beautiful, she was healthy, she was mine, and she looked exactly like me, as I looked like my mommy, and no one even dared to take her away from me.

I named my baby daughter "Joanna" after my mommy ....

XIV

"Herein is our love made perfect, that we may have bold-ness in the day of judgment: because as he is, so are we in this world."   *I John 4:17*

My Mother

EXHAUSTED SITTING HERE in this old worn recliner, not from the long highway trip here or from the hours spent in this hospital room, but from seeing my life, as it was through my buried memories. I looked toward this woman, my mother, and I thanked God for her. Watching her lying there in pain, I knew she, my *mother,* without knowing it, gave me the best gift that I would ever need. The gift of learning how to survive. And I began to cry, but not to myself this time. I did not let the tears build up within my eyes like years gone past; I let the tears flood my face like an open water faucet. The flood of tears from years ago poured down my face and drenched by blouse, cleansing my soul and heart, and washed away the hurt and pain, the anger and hatred of yesterday. And I smiled down at her and thanked God for her and that I had survived.

I did survive the physical abuse, and molestation from what everyone thought to be a nice old man, at the age of

73

three years old. And I survived being raped repeatedly by a male family member who came to stay at our house and was allowed to sleep in my bed at the age of five years. I survived the drunken rampages of an alcoholic man who put a roof over my head, food in my mouth and clothes on my back. Yes, I did survive and graduate from high school at seventeen years old and seven months pregnant. I also survived growing up without my real mommy and daddy.

I was raised by this woman, my mother, and slowly grew to love her as my mother. Although it took me until the age of twenty-three years old before I would call her mother, I did and will always know her as *MOTHER*.

Not having known what real love or happiness even meant made it hard for me to learn to live with it, once it came along. Having had to watch and listen through the years while my mother was being abused, degraded and beaten by her husband, I distrusted and hated men, and what I thought they stood for. Through it all, my mother struggled to care for my baby brother and me as best she could. My mother was not angry or mad at me, as I thought. I know now that she did not hate me, but was lost in her own shame. Ashamed that we, her children, had to watch and hear the things said and done to her and that there was nothing she felt she could do. That look she sometimes gave me was a lesson somehow for me to remember that that was not what I ever wanted to happen to me in my life, or to any child that I might have of my own. Problems, trials and tribulations faced in the past, and the pain and suffering from long ago have made me, if not wiser, a stronger person today. I know there will always be trials and tribulations, and I know now, from having learned in the past, that you may not always have a real or biological mommy and daddy to love you. You may not have someone to run to for help. Sometimes there are people without any blood relation to you at all, who can and will love you as their own, as if you were their family. I know now that my family was very different in many ways from other families, and most probably dysfunctional for the most part. It has taken a long time for me to get to this point, but I don't hate any of them anymore, and I will always love "J'sol," *this woman, my mother.*

My mother passed away peacefully in her sleep, with no one by her side, on a quiet Sunday morning, after I left her in that hospital room, in that place in Kansas that I called home ....

XV

"Brethren, I count not myself to have apprehended: but this one I do forgetting those things which are behind, and reaching forth unto those things which are before."
— *Philippians 3:13*

Missing Pieces

LOSING ANOTHER PARENT as an adult proved to be just as hard as when I was a child. The angry feeling of being left alone again washed over me like a premature shower of a post-menopausal night sweat. I hated that feeling and my mother also, for not trusting in me enough to handle how sick she was. I felt cheated in not being able to have spent more time, and done more, and most of all to have told her just how much I truly loved her. Death had slowly invaded her frail body over the years, and then with an angry vengeance set its weapon of mass destruction within the core of her body and delivered the final blow that took her life.

Doctors could not rationalize to her son or to me a reasonable understanding of how she withstood the pain of the cancer for as long as she had. There were no complaints from her; even at the very end she tried to not let it be known to us the pain she was in, by quieting the

77

moans with a tissue held to her mouth, as if she were merely covering a cough full of germs. And in her painful suffering, she still was thinking of her children, by not wanting to see us upset or sad in her last days, so she endured the pain quietly to herself. Just as she had endured other pains during her life that made this pain of death seem probably like a bed of red roses. Yet, those thorns from the red roses were as a continuous reminder of her abusive life each time they pricked at her insides. A life that was as a garden gone too long unattended, and overgrown with weeds of abuse. This woman, my mother, was like a red rose grown full bloom with age. She was pale in her shade of love and beauty, caused from the lack of identity due to abusive hands. Yet, through the years of careful self-nurturing after the death of those abusive hands, she came into her own light, full of love and hope to become the beautiful rose she was always meant to be. The time for her was not soon enough because the many harsh seasons of abusive neglect slowly dried and withered her red rose petals back into seedless dust of pain …

Sorting through all the papers and packing boxes of clothes after my mother's death, my daughters and I came across an old brown folder. It looked to be full of junk papers, but once pulling everything out, we were surprised to see the contents. There were old childhood drawings from her children and grandchildren that she had kept through the years. There were old newspaper articles when I won the fastest time in the sixth grade track meet, along with the ribbons attached. There were old perfect attendance and penmanship awards, and all the childhood memorabilia that parents keep of their children throughout their childhood in school. There were old school pictures of myself and my baby brother and of her son, along with letters and cards over the years that had been sent to her on Mother's Day, her many birthdays, along with dried rose petals from the many flowers sent by her son and me. My heart ached as I thought of how much she loved and cared enough to keep all of this stuff.

Selecting one of the tattered and yellow faded papers, I noticed that it was one of my eldest daughters, Joanna. As I read it, I could feel the tears sting my eyes, and I knew that I had to find that missing piece in my life ...

My life is like a puzzle
And she is the missing piece.
Others have tried to fill the void,
But the gap still remains.
Just when I settle for second best,
The picture unlinks again.
Why is this such a painstaking task?
I've put one together before.
Where is she?
No, that's not it.
Does she know there's a piece missing, too?
Something so small, yet can be so big.
So many questions,
So many pieces,
A life left incomplete,
A puzzle left unfinished.

EPILOGUE

THE DEATH OF my mother helped me to decide that it was time to find out about my real mother and her family. The burnt image filed in the memory section of my mind was the only picture of my mommy that I possessed. She was sleeping with one eye open and one eye closed watching over us as a guardian angel would, until the men in the white coats took her away. It was now time for me to process that image as hard copy. So now my true journey into my past begins, developed from memories into an unexpected reality.

I think of myself as a feather unknowingly lost from the wing of some migrant bird that is floating through the air. Long ago I felt like a feather, lost and separated, but unique in my own way. Knowing that once ago as a feather, I was part of a graceful bird that soared through the air mighty and proud. I am one of the many feathers that formed part of that cloak of protection, warmth and comfort for that bird when gathered together as one.

I will one day find that bird that lost its feather that I am a part of, and no longer be just another one of the lost feathers ....

.